Dear Parent:
Your child's love of reading starts here!

Every child learns to read in a different way and at his or her own speed. Some go back and forth between reading levels and read favorite books again and again. Others read through each level in order. You can help your young reader improve and become more confident by encouraging his or her own interests and abilities. From books your child reads with you to the first books he or she reads alone, there are I Can Read Books for every stage of reading:

SHARED READING
Basic language, word repetition, and whimsical illustrations, ideal for sharing with your emergent reader

BEGINNING READING
Short sentences, familiar words, and simple concepts for children eager to read on their own

READING WITH HELP
Engaging stories, longer sentences, and language play for developing readers

READING ALONE
Complex plots, challenging vocabulary, and high-interest topics for the independent reader

ADVANCED READING
Short paragraphs, chapters, and exciting themes for the perfect bridge to chapter books

I Can Read Books have introduced children to the joy of reading since 1957. Featuring award-winning authors and illustrators and a fabulous cast of beloved characters, I Can Read Books set the standard for beginning readers.

A lifetime of discovery begins with the magical words **"I Can Read!"**

Visit www.icanread.com for information
on enriching your child's reading experience.

I Can Read Book® is a trademark of HarperCollins Publishers.

The Berenstain Bears Story Collection
Copyright © 2016 by Berenstain Publishing, Inc.
All rights reserved.

The Berenstain Bears' New Pup
Copyright © 2005 by Berenstain Bears, Inc.

The Berenstain Bears' Sleepover
Copyright © 2009 by Berenstain Bears, Inc.

The Berenstain Bears' Class Trip
Copyright © 2009 by Berenstain Bears, Inc.

The Berenstain Bears Clean House
Copyright © 2005 by Berenstain Bears, Inc.

The Berenstain Bears' Lemonade Stand
Copyright © 2014 by Berenstain Publishing, Inc.

Manufactured in China. No part of this book may be used or reproduced in any manner whatsoever without written
permission except in the case of brief quotations embodied in critical articles and reviews. For information address
HarperCollins Children's Books, a division of HarperCollins Publishers, 195 Broadway, New York, NY 10007.

ISBN 978-0-06-246397-5

15 16 17 18 19 SCP 10 9 8 7 6 5 4 3 2 1

❖

First Edition

I Can Read!

BEGINNING **1** READING

The Berenstain Bears®
Story Collection

By Stan & Jan Berenstain
with Mike Berenstain

HARPER

An Imprint of HarperCollins Publishers

Contents

The Berenstain Bears'
New Pup

Stan & Jan Berenstain

One day Mama and the cubs
went to Farmer Ben's farm.
They went there to buy
some fresh eggs.

"Look!" said Brother. "There is a
sign on Farmer Ben's barn door."
The sign said PUPS FOR SALE!
"Hmm," said Mama.
"Farmer Ben's dog, Queenie,
must have had pups."

"Oh, Mama!" said Sister.

"May we have one? May we?

May we? Please?"

"We came to buy eggs," said Mama.

"Not a pup."

Farmer Ben was in the barn.

So was his dog, Queenie.

Queenie was in a box with her pups.

There were many pups.

Some of her pups were having lunch.

Some were sleeping.

One of them was playing

with a piece of straw.

"Oh," said Sister.

"I want that one!

He is so cute."

"That one is a she," said Farmer Ben.

"How can you tell?" asked Brother.

"There are ways," said Farmer Ben.

"Now, cubs," said Mama,
"buying eggs is one thing.
Buying a pup is quite another."

"Oh, Mama," said the cubs,

"may we have her?

May we? May we? Please?"

"A pup is not just something

you have," said Mama.

"A pup is something

you have to take care of."

"We will take care of her!"

said the cubs.

"A pup is something you have to clean up after," said Mama. "We will clean up after her," said the cubs.

"A pup likes to get into things,"
said Mama.

"We will watch her every second!"
said the cubs.

Farmer Ben picked up the pup

that was playing with the straw.

He put her in Mama's hands.

The pup looked into Mama's eyes.

The pup licked Mama's nose.

The pup wagged her tail…

and Mama's heart melted!

On the way home,

they named the pup Little Lady.

They named her "little"

because she was little.

They named her "lady"

because she was a she.

"Yum!" said Papa Bear
when they got home.
"A dozen farm-fresh eggs!"
"And one farm-fresh pup!"
said Sister Bear.

Mama was right about Little Lady.

She did have to be cleaned up after.

She left a puddle in one corner…

and a calling card in another.

And she did like to get into things.

She got into Mama's baking flour.

Cough! Cough! Cough!

She got into Papa's fishing tackle.

What a tangle!

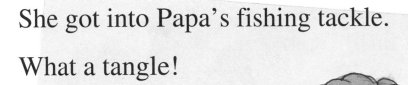

She got into Farmer Ben's

farm-fresh eggs.

What a mess!

"Hmm," said Mama.

"I am going back to Farmer Ben's."

"You're not going to take Little Lady back to Farmer Ben's?" cried Sister.

"No," said Mama.

"I am just going to get another dozen eggs."

The Berenstain Bears' SLEEPOVER

Jan and Mike Berenstain

Sister and Brother Bear were having
a sleepover.

Lizzy and Barry Bruin were
Sister's and Brother's best friends.
They were going to spend the night.

Lizzy and Barry's parents brought them
to the Bears' tree house.

"I hope Lizzy and Barry sleep well
tonight," said Mrs. Bruin.

"We'll make sure they don't stay up
too late," said Mama Bear.

Lizzy and Barry put their things
in Sister and Brother's room.
Then they all had dinner.

After dinner the cubs played

a game of Bearopoly.

Lizzy was winning, and soon owned

most of the tree houses.

The other cubs gave up.

Next, they watched a movie.

It was about a wizard.

The wizard had a magic cape.

No one could see him.

It was neat!

The cubs decided to put on

their own magic show.

They got costumes out of the attic.

The audience was Mama, Papa, and Honey.

The show went well until Barry tripped

on his magic cape.

He knocked over Brother, Sister, and Lizzy!

They laughed and laughed.

"The show is over!" said Mama.

"Time for bed."

The cubs put on their pajamas,

washed up, and brushed their teeth.

Mama and Papa read them

a bedtime story and tucked them in.

"Goodnight, everyone," said Mama,
turning out the lights.

Mama and Papa went to bed

and were soon asleep.

But the cubs were not at all sleepy.

Brother got out his flashlight.

"Let's tell spooky stories!" he said.

Mama woke up.

She thought she heard something.

She woke Papa and they went

to the cubs' room.

Sister and Lizzy were hiding under
the covers.

Brother and Barry seemed to be sleeping.

"What is going on here?" asked Papa.

"Brother was telling a spooky story,"
said Sister,

"and Lizzy got scared and yelled."

"That's enough spooky stories," said Mama.
"Now everyone go to sleep!"

Mama and Papa went back to bed.

Mama heard something again.

She woke Papa and they went

downstairs.

They found the cubs in the kitchen
eating snacks.

"It is too late for snacks," Mama said.

"Back to bed!"

Mama and Papa went back to bed again.

But Mama heard a sound in the bathroom.

She woke Papa.

They found Sister and Lizzy
putting on Mama's lipstick.
Brother and Barry were covered in
Papa's shaving cream.
"That's enough of that!" said Mama.
"Back to bed!"

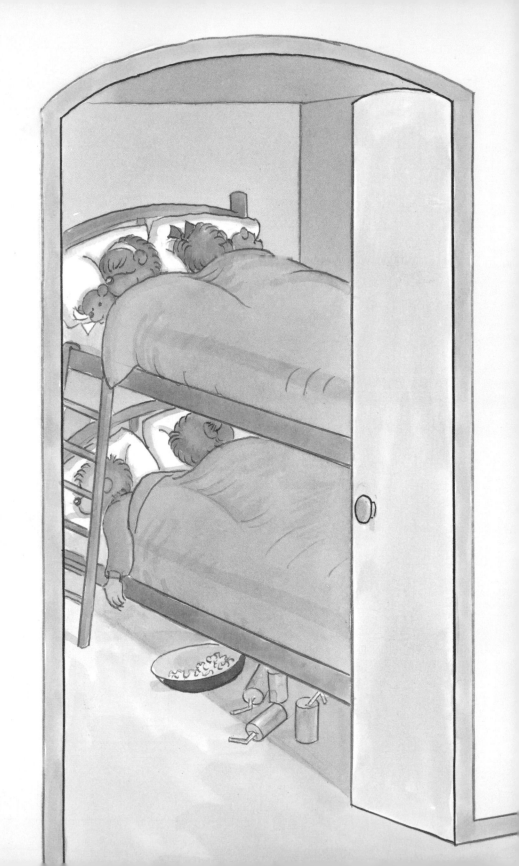

Now the cubs were worn out.

They went right to sleep.

Mama and Papa sat outside

the cubs' room all night.

They did not get much sleep.

The next morning the cubs slept late.

At eleven o'clock, Mr. and Mrs. Bruin
came to pick up Lizzy and Barry.
"I was so worried about them!"
said Mrs. Bruin.
"I didn't sleep a wink all night!"
"Neither did we," said Papa,
his eyes closing.

After Lizzy and Barry went home,

Mama and Papa sat down on the sofa.

They were soon asleep.

It was Mama and Papa's turn for a sleepover!

The Berenstain Bears'
Class Trip

Jan & Mike Berenstain

Brother Bear's class is going on a trip.

The class is going to a honey farm.

Mama and Papa Bear are
teacher's helpers on the trip.

"Mmm," says Papa Bear, licking his lips.

"I hope they give out free samples."

"I am sure they do," says Mama Bear.

Sister Bear is going, too.

There is an extra seat on the bus

next to Teacher Bob.

Honey Bear will stay at home
with Gramps and Gran.

The bus is on its way.

"Let's all sing!" says Cousin Fred.

"Ninety-nine jars of honey on the wall . . ."

sings the class.

Papa Bear joins in.

"Are we almost there?" asks Sister.

"Almost!" answers Papa.

They see a sign:

BEAR COUNTRY HONEY FARM, NEXT EXIT.

"Hooray!" yells the class.

Brother Bear sniffs the air.

"Smell that?" he says. "Honey!"

They all take a deep breath.

"*Mmm!*" They sigh.

"I can almost taste that honey now,"
says Papa, licking his lips again.
"Look! We are here!" says Sister.

They all get off the bus.

Teacher Bob leads the way.

They see a huge field of beehives.

The sound of buzzing bees fills the air.

"Over there is the clover field,"

says Teacher Bob.

"Thousands of bees gather nectar there.

They bring it back to the hives

and make it into honey."

"How do they do that?" asks Brother.

"Look," says Teacher Bob.

He points to a hive.

"You can see for yourself."

One of the hives has a glass side.

The cubs can see the bees making honey.

"See that big bee?" says Papa.

"That is the queen."

"Correct," says Teacher Bob.

"All the others are her children."

"Wow," says Sister.

"She has more children

than the Old Bear in the Shoe!"

"How do you get the honey
out of the hive?" asks Brother.
"I'll show you," says Papa.
He lifts the lid of a hive.

"No! No!" says Teacher Bob.
A huge cloud of bees flies out.

"Follow me!" shouts Teacher Bob.

All the bears run into the honey barn.

Teacher Bob slams the door shut
just in time.

"Now you will see the correct way
to get the honey out," he says.

The cubs look out the window.

Beekeepers are gathering honey.

They wear special suits and hats

to keep from getting stung.

First, the beekeepers blow smoke into
the hives to make the bees sleepy.
Then they lift out the honeycombs.

They bring the honeycombs into the barn.

They put them on a big wheel.

They turn the crank.

Golden honey pours into a big vat.

Papa cannot wait to taste the honey.

He leans over too far and gets

honey all over himself.

"While Papa Bear is getting cleaned up, you may all have some honey samples," says Teacher Bob.

"Yea!" cry the cubs.

The class is back on the bus
heading home.

Mama Bear says, "I saved a honey
sample for you, Papa dear."

"No, thank you," says Papa.

"I have already had my sample!"

The Berenstain Bears
CLEAN HOUSE

By Stan & Jan Berenstain

"It is spring," said Mama Bear.

"It is time to clean our house."

"I will help," said Papa.

"I will help," said Brother.

"I will help," said Sister.

"Good," said Mama.

"We will clean our house
from the top to the bottom,
from the bottom to the top."

They started at the bottom.

"My goodness," said Mama.

"There are too many things.

It is hard to clean with so many things."

"We will have a yard sale," said Papa.

"We will put some in the yard."

"This old fish," said Brother.

"It is dusty."

"This stuffed owl," said Sister.

"It is musty."

"This old fishing pole,"
said Mama.
"It is bent."

"Those are my things,"
said Papa.
"But it is spring.
We must clean house.
I will put them
in the yard."

They went upstairs
to the living room.

"There are too many things," said Papa.
"We must put some in the yard,"
said Mama.

"This old lamp," said Brother.

"It has a crack."

"This old pillow," said Sister.

"It has a spot on the back."

"This old stool," said Papa.

"It has a tear."

"Those are my things,"
said Mama.
"But I will put them
in the yard."

Then they went upstairs

Brother and Sister's room

had many, many things.

"My goodness!" said Mama.

"There are too many things in this room.

We must put some in the yard."

"This baseball bat," said Papa.

"It is split."

"This teddy bear," said Mama.

"The stuffing is coming out of it."

"These old games
and toys," said Papa.
"They would be fun
for other girls and boys."

"Those are our things,"
said Brother and Sister.
"We will put them
in the yard."

"Yes, it is spring," said Mama.

"We must clean our house

from the top to the bottom,

from the bottom to the top."

But there was something they forgot!

They forgot the attic!

"My goodness!" said Mama.

"We forgot the attic."

They went up to the attic.

It was bad.

"My goodness!" said Mama.

"There are too many things!"

"Yes," said Papa.

"Many too many to put in the yard."

They went downstairs.

They went out to
the yard.

118

They made a sign.

It said YARD SALE TODAY.

They looked at the things
they put in the yard.

"This is hard," said Papa.
"I love those things
I put in the yard."

"This is hard," said Mama.

"I love those things

I put in the yard."

"This is hard,"

said Brother and Sister.

"We love those things

we put in the yard."

They took them up
to the attic.

They put them with the other
old things they loved.

"We have done our job," said Mama.

"But we are not done," said Brother.
"We have not cleaned the attic," said
Sister.

"We are done," said Mama.

"But the attic will not go away.

We will clean the attic

another day."

The Berenstain Bears' Lemonade Stand

Mike Berenstain

Based on the characters created by Stan and Jan Berenstain

It is a hot day.

Brother, Sister, and Honey Bear

play outside.

Mama brings them lemonade.

Ahh! It is good.

Mailbear Bob comes by.

He is very hot.

"May I have some

lemonade?" he asks.

"I will give you a quarter."

Mailbear Bob drinks the lemonade.

Ahh! It is good.

"Here is your quarter," he says.

"Let's sell more lemonade,"
says Brother.

The cubs set up a lemonade stand.

They make a sign:

"Lemonade—25 cents."

Some bears are mowing

the lawn next door.

They are very hot.

They see the lemonade stand.

"We would like some lemonade,"
say the lawn bears.

They drink it down.

Ahh! It is good.

Their neighbor comes outside.

"I am having a party," she says.

"My guests will all want

lemonade."

Her guests arrive.

They all drink lemonade.

Ahh! It is good.

Some other neighbors come outside.

They want lemonade, too.

But the cubs are running out of

lemonade.

"Don't worry!" say the neighbors.

"We will help."

They bring out more drinks.

They bring out food to eat.

Some cubs come by.

"A block party!" they say.

They start to play music.

They start to dance.

It is a big party!

Farmer Ben sees the party.

He has a load of things from his farm.

He starts to sell fruit and other good things.

It is getting dark.

How will the party end?

Grizzly Gus has fireworks.

He sets them off.

They are very pretty!

The party is over.

Everyone goes home.

The cubs take down their
lemonade stand.
They go inside.
They are very tired.
They are very hot.

Mama brings them lemonade.

Ahh! It is good.

"That will be twenty-five cents,"

says Mama.

They all laugh at Mama's joke!